Little Horrors

Tikki the Tricky Pixie

Titles in the Series

Little Horrors

Tikki the Tricky Pixie

Tiffany Mandrake

Illustrated by Martin Chatterton

LITTLE HARE

www.littleharebooks.com

Little Hare Books
8/21 Mary Street, Surry Hills
NSW 2010 AUSTRALIA

www.littleharebooks.com

National Library of Australia
Cataloguing-in-Publication entry

Mandrake, Tiffany.

Tikki the tricky pixie / Tiffany Mandrake;
illustrator, Martin Chatterton.

978 1 921541 32 2 (pbk.)

Mandrake, Tiffany. Little horrors; 4.

For primary school age.

Pixies—Juvenile fiction.

Chatterton, Martin.

A823.3

Cover design by Martin Chatterton
Set in 16/22 pt Bembo by Clinton Ellicott
Printed by WKT Company Limited
Printed in Shenzhen, Guangdong Province, China, December 2009

5 4 3 2 1

Contents

For all you little horrors out there

—TM

To Sophie Chat: What an amazing effort this year!

—MC

A Note from Tiffany Mandrake

Psst, this is me, Tiffany Mandrake, speaking to you from my cosy, creepy cottage in the grounds of Hags' Abademy of Badness. The Abademy is a place where bad fairies go to study how to be truly bad. It's not far from where you live, but you probably won't see it. The fairy-breed use special spells to make sure you don't.

It is run by three water hags, Maggie Nabbie, Auld Anni and Kirsty Breeks. They started the

Abademy because too many fairies were doing sweet deeds.

Sweet deeds are not always good deeds, and the world needs a bit of honest badness for balance. Otherwise, we humans get slack and lazy. The Abademy provides that balance. To enter the Abademy, young fairies must earn a Badge of Badness.

This is the story of one tricky pixie named Tikki Flicker, and what she did in Pisky Marsh.

I promised not to tell anyone . . . but you can keep a secret, can't you?

Sure you can.

So listen . . . And remember, not a word to anyone!

1. A Hag in the Marsh

Tikki Flicker was in trouble for planting forget-me-nots in Pisky Marsh.

'Don't *do* that, Tikki Flicker!' grumbled Uncle Sedge. 'Remember the Pixie Code—*Good pixies mind the marsh.*'

Tikki giggled. 'But Uncle Sedge, I'm a *bad* pixie. Putting plants where they annoy you is my most favourite bit of badness.'

'Nonsense,' said her uncle. He snorted. 'Bad pixie indeed! *Hmph!*'

Tikki flickered away.* 'I am *so* a bad pixie,' she said.

She hid in her favourite look-see tree and spied on the old pixie as he poked the forget-me-not with a stick. 'Get out of there!' he scolded it. 'You have no right to be in this marsh. Get back to the garden where you belong!' The forget-me-not went on blooming. Uncle Sedge couldn't undo Tikki's magic.

'I don't understand that pest of a pixie,' muttered Uncle Sedge, tugging up the forget-me-not by hand.

'Aye, that's plain to see,' said a cheerful voice.

Tikki almost fell from the tree as a

---

*Flickering is the way young pixies get about.

water hag appeared. She was tall and thin, and dressed in faded tartan tatters.

'It's been a wee while since we met, Sedge Withy,' said the hag.

'Go away, Auld Anni,' said Sedge.

'There's a fine welcome,' said Anni.

Sedge puffed out his bony chest. 'As Warden of Pisky Marsh, I keep the marsh free of troublemakers.' He glowered at Anni. 'That means bad fairies, feral flowers and dryfeet.'

'Dryfeet? You mean humans! What have you got against them?' wondered Anni.

'Nothing, if they stay out of my marsh,' growled Sedge. 'They scare my birds, they splatter my paths and they tramp through my pixie village. They let their garden flowers escape, and they dig up my bog plants.'

In the look-see tree, Tikki sighed.
Uncle Sedge was so boring. She listened
as the hag spoke again.

'Aye, but I am here about your niece,
Tikki Flicker.'

'Why?' said Uncle Sedge, scowling so
much his face looked like a walnut shell.

'She's a bad fairy,' said Anni.

'Nonsense,' Uncle Sedge said.

Anni ticked off points on her gleaming
green fingernails. 'You don't understand
her. She doesn't fit in. She makes

mischief. She is noisy, troublesome, scurrysome, bothersome, and hurrysome.'

Sedge's scowl grew until his chin almost met his nose. 'Bad fairies are bad news,' he said.

'There's nothing wrong with bad fairies,' retorted the hag. 'They add spice to life. *But*, the young ones need proper schooling.'

Tikki almost fell out of the look-see tree in excitement. This hag knew Tikki was a bad fairy and she didn't seem to mind!

'She gets schooling,' said Uncle Sedge.

'But does she listen?' said the hag dryly.

'Hurrumph!' muttered Uncle Sedge.

'You know,' said the hag, 'there's a school for bad fairies where Tikki would belong.'

Tikki almost cheered. Going to a special school for bad fairies would be *so* much better than being told what to do by Uncle Sedge!

But Uncle Sedge growled, 'Tikki will stay in the marsh, and learn to mind it like a good pixie. She's *not* a bad fairy.'

'What do the other pixies think?' asked the hag.

'They think the same as me, and so should Tikki. Go away, hag.' Sedge stalked off towards Frog Glade.

'Pish!' said Anni, and marched away.

Tikki felt in her pocket for a golf ball she had stolen from Ballyhaggis Golf Course.★ She tossed it after the hag to get her attention, but Auld Anni had gone.

★*Golf balls often vanish from golf courses. That's because bad fairies steal them.*

2. The Pixiepackers

Tikki sprang out of the look-see tree and flickered after Uncle Sedge. She had to make him see she belonged at the school for bad fairies! More forget-me-nots popped into bloom in her wake.

She paused to rap on a hollow tree. A tribe of swamp imps lived inside. 'Hey, imps!' Tikki said. 'I'm a really bad fairy! The hag said so!'

The imps stuck out their tongues and waggled their fingers in their ears. Tikki blew a loud, rude raspberry.

'*Ooo-er!*' said the imps, and ducked back into their tree.

Tikki found her uncle tugging up another forget-me-not. She danced about him. 'I *am* a bad fairy!' she whooped. 'You have to let me go to that school! The hag said——'

Uncle Sedge glared at her. 'Forget what she said. I'll hear no more about it. And what's the meaning of *this*?' He plucked one of Tikki's golf balls from a clump of marsh marigold. 'Those dryfeet again, I suppose.'

'That's mine,' said Tikki. She reached for the ball, but Sedge dropped it into his pouch. 'But Uncle Sedge!' pleaded Tikki. 'I'd fit in at that school——'

'Nonsense,' snapped Sedge. He stamped away.

Tikki stared after him. It wasn't fair! He was spoiling her chance to go to a real school, *and* he'd taken her golf ball. She decided to go to the golf course and steal some more. She wasn't allowed in Ballyhaggis Village, but so what? She *was* a bad fairy, whether Uncle Sedge admitted it or not. If she did something extra bad in the village, he might change his mind.

Frog Glade was on the edge of the marsh, so Tikki kept walking. Beyond lay Ballyhaggis Meadow. The ground was purple with heather and starred with daisies and buttercups.

Tikki poked her pixie boot into the grass and made forget-me-nots grow and bloom. *That* would annoy Uncle Sedge!

Then she swaggered across the meadow to Ballyhaggis Golf Course.

Tikki watched a dryfoot whack a ball down the course. He couldn't see or hear Tikki, because she was wearing her DNM or Don't Notice Me spell.

She flickered ahead and found the ball resting close to the hole. The golfer was about to tap the ball into the hole when Tikki flicked it the other way.

'Did you see that?' gasped the golfer.

'See what?' said his friend.

'That ball! It was right *here*, and now it's over *there*.' He grabbed for it, but Tikki put it in her pocket.

'Huh?' said the golfers, as the ball disappeared.

Tikki went into the village, but teasing dryfeet wasn't as much fun as usual. She needed an extra-special badness to make Uncle Sedge understand. Her mind kept returning to the water hag's offer.

She was about to go home when she saw a dinky cottage painted with red and white spots. Its roof was shaped like a mushroom. Over the door hung a sign.

Pixiepackers' Clubhouse.

Tikki spied through an open window.
Inside the room, she saw five female
dryfeet. They wore green skirts with
jagged hems, and green shirts. Each shirt
had a pink letter P on one pocket, and a
different letter on the other. The biggest
dryfoot was tall and hearty. Her hair was
cut in a blonde fringe and she had big
white teeth. Her extra pocket letter was
an L. The smaller ones had a C, a B, a J
and a G. Tikki noticed C had a blonde
fringe like L, but B had two long black
plaits. J had a bouncy ponytail, and G
had bushy brown hair.

Dryfoot L picked up a green plastic
wand. 'Gather round, Pixiepackers.
It's time for our pixie-dance!' she said.

'Yay, Leader!' called the girls.

*Pixie*packers? They're not pixies! thought Tikki.

Leader frowned. 'Where is Pixie H?'

Pixie C laughed, and flipped her fringe with her finger. 'Hogmanay sneaked out while we sang the Pixiepacker Code.'

'We can't have *that*!' said Leader. 'Pixie H? Where are you hiding?' She clapped her hands. 'Let's find Pixie H.'

The dryfeet flitted about, peering behind curtains and under tables. 'Pixie H! Pix-ie *Aaa-aaa-ch*!' they called.

The search looked like fun, so Tikki decided to join in.

Pixie H was not in the cottage, so everyone, including Tikki, flocked into the garden. The hunt began again.

'Pixie H! Pix-ie *Aaa-aaa-ch*!'

Some twigs fell from a tree near Tikki. She looked up, straight at a dryfoot boy.

He was dressed in green like the others, but instead of a skirt he wore shorts. He didn't look happy.

Tikki flickered into the tree and flicked a golf ball at the boy. 'Hello!' she said.

Pixie H jumped. 'Wh-who's there?'

Tikki took off her DNM spell so the boy could see her. That was strictly forbidden. 'Me,' she said.

The boy goggled. 'Where did you come from? What are you meant to be?'

'I'm Tikki Flicker, from Pisky Marsh,' said Tikki. 'They say you're Pixie H. That's silly, 'cos you're not a pixie. *I* am.'

The boy snorted. 'I'm Hogmanay McKay. Of course I'm not a stupid pixie! It's my sister Chrissie's fault. She joined the Pixiepacker Club, and Mam made me join, too. You're not a pixie either. Pixies don't exist.'

Tikki prodded the boy with her finger. 'Do too!'

Hogmanay McKay lost his balance with a startled yelp. Next moment, he was hanging by his hands and feet from the branch.

The yelp attracted the Pixiepackers, who swarmed around the tree.

'*There* you are, Pixie H!' said Leader, pulling him down. 'It's pixie-dance time. Then after that we'll plan our nature study camp in Ballyhaggis Meadow.'

Hogmanay stared around. 'Where's that pixie?'

'What pixie, Pixie H?'

'The green one with fake ears,' Hogmanay said. He pointed into the tree, but Tikki had gone.

3. An Invitation

'Where have you been?' grumbled Uncle Sedge when Tikki returned to the marsh.

'I was cross because you wouldn't let me go to the bad-fairy school, so I went and played with a dryfoot,' said Tikki. 'He was funny, Uncle Sedge. He hung upside down from a tree. Lots of silly dryfeet looked for him, and I helped them look, and——'

'*Nonsense!*' snapped Uncle Sedge. 'As if any good pixies would let dryfeet see them! It's against the rules.'

'But I'm a *bad* pixie!' said Tikki.

'Pixies are not bad,' said Sedge. 'Pixies exist to mind the marsh. Pixies stay away from dryfeet, because dryfeet wreck the marsh.' He stamped away.

Tikki went back to Frog Glade and banged on the swamp imps' hollow tree. 'Come out!' she demanded. 'I really, *really* need your help to make Uncle Sedge understand I'm a bad pixie. He just won't listen to me!'

'Tikki Flicker?' said a voice from above her head.

Tikki looked up at something perched on a branch. 'Who are you?' asked Tikki.

'I am the filly-fae, your fairy fetch,' said the creature.

Tikki flickered into the tree to investigate. The filly-fae looked like a pocket-sized pony with wings. '*Oooh*, pretty!' Tikki said.

The creature swished its tail. 'Critter-fae are not *pretty*,' it said.

'What's a critter-fae? You said you were a filly-fae fairy fetch.'

'Critter-fae are imps with animal DNA,' said the creature. 'I have marsh-pony DNA. There is only one of me in the world. You're a lucky pixie, because I have brought you an invitation from Hags' Abademy of Badness.'

'*Oooh!*' said Tikki. 'Is that the bad fairy school? A water hag tried to tell Uncle Sedge about it today, but he wouldn't listen. He won't even believe I'm a bad fairy.'

'That hag was Auld Anni,' said the

filly-fae. 'She runs the Abademy with Maggie Nabbie and Kirsty Breeks. They sent an invitation for you to take a badness test. If you're bad enough, the hags will award you a Badge of Badness. Then you can go to the Abademy and learn to be worse.'

Tikki sighed. 'Uncle Sedge would never let me go. He thinks all pixies are good, so he can't understand I'm bad.

When I tell him about the bad things
I do, he either thinks I made a mistake,
or says I'm talking nonsense.'

'Then you *need* a Badge of Badness,'
said the filly-fae. 'That's proof of badness
that even Sedge Withy can't ignore.'

The filly-fae gave Tikki a bark strip
with writing on it. Tikki read the
words aloud. '*Are **you** a **bad pixie**? Do you
relish being **really rotten**, **tantalisingly
tricky**, and **mindbogglingly bad**? Answer
Yes or No.*'

Tikki smiled. 'Yes!' she said.

More lines appeared, and Tikki read
on. '*If you answered Yes, you may earn a
Badge of Badness and attend the Hags'
Abademy for further badness training.*'

Tikki leapt down to dance a jig-spell
on a tree stump. A cloud of startled
fireflies appeared in the air.

'Finish reading your invitation,' said the filly-fae.

Tikki read on. *'To qualify for your badge, you must create and perform an act of breathtaking badness. The filly-fae will guide you.'*

The filly-fae landed beside Tikki. 'Can you perform an act of breathtaking badness?' it asked.

'I was *born* to be bad,' said Tikki. 'I'll fit in straight away at this Abademy. I'll show Uncle Sedge once and for all that I'm *right*.'

4. Hogmanay McKay

After Leader pulled him out of the tree, Hogmanay McKay danced around a plastic pixie hat with his sister Chrissie, and her friends Bella, Gretel and Jade. He didn't want to dance around a pixie hat. Leader made him do it.

'Come along, Pixie H!' she boomed in her horribly hearty voice. 'Remember the Pixiepacker Code. *Whenever pixies get*

a chance, they always do the pixie-dance.
Look happy! Pixies are happy! Pixies are
helpful! Pixies are busy! *Real* pixies *love*
to see us following the Pixiepacker Code.'

Hogmanay opened his mouth to say
there were no real pixies. Then he shut
it again. That pointy-eared girl had
appeared out of nowhere, and then
disappeared. What if she *was* a real pixie?

He decided to investigate, as soon as
the stupid Pixiepacker meeting was over.

*

'What bad deed can you do?' asked the
filly-fae.

Tikki sat on the tree stump and swung
her legs. 'I could bother and annoy and
pester,' she said. 'I'm good at that.'

'Not enough!' said the filly-fae. 'You
must think of something big, bad and
bold to impress the hags.'

Tikki tried to think big, but the only bad deeds she knew of were little things she did all the time. She was about to explain this to the filly-fae when someone called her name.

'Tikki Flicker? Where are you?'

The voice sounded grumpy. Voices calling for Tikki usually did sound like that.

'Who's there?' asked the filly-fae, swishing its tail crossly.

'How should I know?' Tikki said.

'Whoever it is appears to know *you*,' said the fetch.

Tikki flickered away to the look-see tree and peered about. Not far away, balanced on a log over the bog, she saw a dryfoot boy dressed in green shorts and a green shirt. Tikki realised he was the same boy she had met earlier.

'Tikki Flicker. Pixie girl. Where are you?' called the boy.

Tikki flickered over to the dryfoot. She looked at his feet, and giggled. 'I should give you a little push,' she said.

'Tikki Flicker!' the boy growled. 'Where are you? It's Hogmanay McKay.'

'Leave that human alone,' said the filly-fae. 'It'll soon go away.'

Tikki balanced beside Hogmanay, and removed her DNM spell. 'Boo!'

Hogmanay staggered, squawked, threw up his arms, and toppled into the bog.

A wave of muddy water splashed about. The filly-fae flew into the air with a startled neigh.

Tikki, still balanced on the log, laughed and laughed. She hugged herself, and rocked back and forth in her pixie boots, fluttering her small green wings.

All around, forget-me-nots sprang into bloom.

Hogmanay McKay floundered, kicking up more mud. 'Help!' he squawked. 'Get me out!'

Tikki stopped laughing. 'Get out by yourself,' she said.

The boy realised he was in no danger. He sat up, and wiped his face with his muddy hands.

Tikki looked at him. 'Get up, Pixie H. It's no fun if you just sit there.'

'Don't call me Pixie H!' grumbled the boy. 'I'm Hogmanay McKay.' He wiped his face again. 'You're Tikki Flicker.'

'Yes,' agreed Tikki. 'This is the filly-fae.' She flickered quickly into the tree. 'Take off your DNM spell so I can show you to Pixie H,' she said to the fetch.

'No,' it said.

'Aw, come on,' wheedled Tikki. 'It would be a big treat for a dryfoot to see someone as special as you.'

'Well . . .' The filly-fae considered. 'All right then,' it decided. It faded into view, then zoomed around the boy's head.

Hogmanay McKay goggled up at the fetch. 'No way!' he said. 'A flying pony-bug!' He got to his feet, pouring muddy water from his pockets, paddled to a bank, sat down, and took off his boots. 'You really are a pixie,' he said. 'Cool!'

5. Plans

Hogmanay McKay stared at the fetch as he tried to clean the mud from his clothes with a handful of grass. 'So, if you're a pixie, and that's a flying pony-bug, does this mean there are *more* things like you?'

Tikki flickered to sit beside him. 'The filly-fae is a special sort of imp. And there are swamp imps at Frog Glade,' she said. 'I'm the only bad pixie around here.'

'Leader says pixies are helpful, friendly and busy,' said Hogmanay.

'That doesn't sound like the pixies I know,' said Tikki. 'They mind the marsh and take care of pixie business. They're not friendly, or kind, and they don't approve of dryfeet like you in the marsh *at all.*' She shrugged. 'Not like bad fairies.'

'What do bad fairies do?'

Tikki sprang up and twirled on her toes. 'We bother and bewilder. We pester and annoy. We keep dryfeet on their toes. Without us, they'd get lazy.'

'That doesn't sound very bad,' said Hogmanay. 'You do push people into the marsh though. That's bad.'

'I didn't push you. I just came when you called.' Tikki giggled. 'If you'd stayed out of Pisky Marsh, then you couldn't have fallen into it.'

'I'd like to push Leader and my sister Chrissie into the marsh,' grumbled Hogmanay. 'Then I could stop going to Pixiepacker Club.'

'Why do you go, if you don't like it?'

'Mam says I have to.' Hogmanay shuddered. 'We're going on a Pixiepacker camp on Friday. It'll be horrible. I'll be stuck with loads of stupid girls, dancing about and seeing good in everything.'

Suddenly, Tikki had an idea. 'If the camp's in the marsh, I could make it *really* horrible.'

'But the camp won't be in the marsh,' said Hogmanay. 'It's going to be in Ballyhaggis Meadow.'

'What if there were big bitey beetles in the meadow?' asked Tikki.

'There are no big bitey beetles in Ballyhaggis Meadow,' said Hogmanay.

'Not yet,' said Tikki. 'But I can arrange for some to be there on Friday. If Leader and the other dryfeet see bitey beetles in the meadow, they'll run like rabbits into the marsh.'

Hogmanay smiled. 'You *are* bad, aren't you?'

Tikki nodded. 'Of course. I'm a bad fairy.'

'Why do you want to help me, if you're bad?'

'I like you. But mainly, I need to perform an act of breathtaking badness so I can win a Badge of Badness. Then I can go to the Abademy of Badness to learn to be worse,' explained Tikki. 'To do *that*, I need to prove to my silly old uncle that I really *am* a bad fairy. This can be my act. Let's plan.'

*

Half an hour later, the boy and the pixie parted company. Before Hogmanay McKay went home, Tikki de-mudded his Pixiepacker uniform with a jig-spell so he wouldn't be in trouble.

'Bad fairies don't clean clothes,' said the filly-fae. 'That's a house-brownie's job.'★

Tikki grinned. 'But I like Hogmanay McKay. And his mother can't be cross with him, or else he won't be allowed to come on the camp on Friday. My bad deed will never work without him. Come on, Fiffy. Let's visit the swamp imps.'

Tikki flickered off to Frog Glade, and put her mouth to the hollow in the tree. 'Swamp imps, are you in there?'

★*Brownies are fairy-breed. They live in houses and clean things. They are good fairies, but they expect to be paid with milk.*

The imps squeaked disagreeably.
'You're a pixie. We don't like pixies.'

'We don't like *anybody*,' said one.

'We're bad, we are,' said another.

'Brilliant!' said Tikki. 'Will you be very, very bad for me?'

'No,' said the first imp. 'We don't like you.'

'Oh,' said Tikki. She winked at the filly-fae. 'Obviously, they couldn't do it, Fiffy,' she said loudly. 'Pretending to be big bitey beetles is *far* too difficult for little swamp imps. We'll have to find someone badder.'

She held her breath as the imps squeaked indignantly. Then the leader popped its head out of the hollow. 'Who says we can't do it, pixie?' it said. 'Swamp imps are clever. We can do anything we choose!'

'OK then,' said Tikki. 'I'll give you a chance to prove it.'

6. Bitey Beetles

On Friday, the Pixiepackers marched into Ballyhaggis Meadow, wearing their uniforms, and carrying rucksacks. As they marched, they sang the Pixiepacker Code. Leader marked the beat with her green plastic wand.

'Pixiepackers smile and sing. They see good in everything. Pixiepackers never whine. They always have a lovely time. Pixiepackers are

good as gold. They do exactly as they're told.
Pixiepackers are nature lovers, kind to pets and
all the others! Whenever pixies get a chance,
they always do the pixie-dance.'

*

In Pisky Marsh, Uncle Sedge's pointed
ears pricked up with outrage. He climbed
into Tikki's look-see tree to see what was
going on.

There were dryfeet in the meadow,
right next to Pisky Marsh! 'Shoo! Scat!'
muttered Sedge, but the dryfeet marched
into the centre of the meadow, then
stopped among the heathery grass.

The tallest dryfoot waved a green stick.
'Set up camp, Pixiepackers. Divide
yourselves into teams and pitch those
tents.'

Sedge watched with horror. 'Go *away*!'
he said.

'*Oooh!* It's the Pixiepackers! My favourite dryfeet *ever*,' said Tikki, landing beside him on the branch.

Sedge snarled at her. 'How do you know who they are?'

Tikki looked down at the Pixiepackers with glee. 'Why are you so upset, Uncle Sedge?'

'I want those dryfeet out of the meadow,' said Sedge. 'They're too close to the marsh. Next thing, they'll be digging up my bog plants! Now *mind the marsh* and get rid of them, Tikki.'

'Why don't you?' Tikki asked.

'I'm taking a forget-me-not squad to Pisky Island,' said Sedge. 'The pestiferous plants are growing there again.'

Tikki flickered to Frog Glade with the filly-fae, and rapped on the hollow tree. 'Are you ready?' she asked.

There was no reply, but Tikki heard
the swamp imps sizzling with glee.

'Come into the meadow, and wait for
my signal,' she said.

Tikki strolled over to where the four
Pixiepacker girls were setting up tents.
Hogmanay McKay was pretending to help.

'Check the ropes holding up that tent,
Pixie H!' said Leader.

Hogmanay checked the ropes. 'They're
loose,' he said. Tikki saw that was true,
because Hogmanay had loosened them.

'Tighten them, Pixie H,' said Leader.

Hogmanay tied the ropes into
complicated knots.

Tikki came up beside him, and slipped
off her DNM spell. 'Hello!' She poked
him with her finger. Then she turned and
nodded to the imps.

Hogmanay jumped. '*There* you are!

Where are the big bitey beetles you promised?'

Tikki pointed to his boot. 'There's one.'

Hogmanay pulled back his foot. On the boot perched what looked like a fat green beetle.★ It had red horns and fangs.

'Wow!' Hogmanay admired the beetle for a moment. Then he kicked out, flicking the creature off his toe. The bitey beetle sailed through the air, and landed on Hogmanay's blonde-haired sister, Chrissie, who was bending over a tent peg. It gnashed its fangs. Chrissie didn't notice, but her bushy-haired friend, Gretel, spotted the beetle and squealed.

'What's all the fuss, Pixie G?' asked Leader.

'There's a *beetle* on Chrissie!'

★*Imps can look any way they want.*

'That's nothing to squeal about,' said Leader. 'Let's practise nature study. Remember the Pixiepacker Code! *Pixiepackers are nature lovers, kind to pets and all the others.*'

'What a big beetle!' said the girl called Jade, who had been pitching another tent. She tossed her ponytail over her shoulder.

'It's a bitey beetle,' said Hogmanay. He looked for Tikki, but she'd disappeared.

'Beetles around here don't bite, Pixie H,' said Leader.

'I think this one does,' said Hogmanay, as the beetle snapped its fangs.

Chrissie spun round twice, trying to see her own back. Leader stopped her, and bent to examine the beetle. The beetle examined Leader. Then it spread its green wings and buzzed up to perch on Leader's nose.

Leader crossed her eyes, and peered at her own nose. 'My word, Pixiepackers, it *is* a big beetle!' She carefully removed the beetle. 'Maybe it's a *magic* beetle.'

The Pixiepacker girls crowded round Leader. They peered into her cupped hands.

'It's *pretty*,' said the fourth girl, Bella.

'I think it might be a Triceratops Beetle. I'll look it up in my *Beetlepedia*.'

'It's a beautiful beetle,' said Jade. 'I think it belongs to a little pixie girl.'

The beetle peered up at the Pixiepackers and snapped its jaws with delight. It wasn't every day that an imp got told it was beautiful.

Things weren't working out as Tikki had expected, but she waved her hands, giving the signal for the swamp imps to swarm.

Hogmanay put his hand to his ear. 'What's that noise?'

'I can't hear anything, Pixie H,' said Leader, admiring the beetle-imp. But at that moment she heard a low, whining hum. She glanced up and saw the whole tribe of imps whirring over the meadow. 'Look!' she cried. 'Here come *more* lovely beetles. Quick, Pixiepackers, see how many specimens you can collect! We'll look them up in Pixie B's *Beetlepedia*.'

Tikki looked proudly at the filly-fae. 'Now they'll run like rabbits, into the marsh. Uncle Sedge will be *furious*. He'll *have* to admit I'm bad then, won't he?' she said.

7. Pixiepackers are Nature Lovers . . .

'Tikki Flicker!' hissed Hogmanay. 'Where are you?'

'Right here,' said Tikki.

Hogmanay peered around. 'I can't see you.' He watched as the air seemed to shiver. A dim Tikki-shaped outline appeared. He scowled. 'You said you'd scare everyone with beetles. They're not scared.' He pointed to where the

Pixiepackers darted about the meadow, gently catching beetles in their hands.

'They do nature study,' said Hogmanay. 'The Pixiepacker Code says they have to love nature. Remember?'

In a cross voice he sang, *'Pixiepackers smile and sing. They see good in everything.'* Hogmanay stopped singing and looked at Tikki. 'That's the first bit. It carries on like this,' he said, and sang *'. . . Pixiepackers never whine. They always have a lovely time.'*

Hogmanay took a deep breath. 'The end goes like this,' he said, and sang *'. . . Pixiepackers are good as gold. They do exactly as they're told. Pixiepackers are nature lovers, kind to pets and all the others!'*

Tikki was about to answer when Leader looked up from her beetle lesson.

'Very *good*, Pixie H, but you're missing out on seeing these beautiful beetles.'

'*Do* something,' Hogmanay hissed at Tikki before he sulked off to admire the still-preening beetle-imps. 'Gee, they're ugly,' he said. 'Look at those *fangs*!'

'Pixie H! Nature is *beautiful*,' said Leader. 'Pixiepackers *love* nature.'

Tikki looked sideways at the filly-fae, which was balanced on her shoulder. 'Why aren't those beetles biting?'

'I think the swamp imps like being told how beautiful they are,' said the filly-fae. 'Come on, Tikki Flicker! Think of something!'

Tikki picked a long sprig of heather, then extended her DNM spell to cover it. 'You can help, Fiffy,' she said. 'I'll flick some of the dryfeet with this, you flick the others. Use your tail!'

Without waiting for the fetch to answer,
Tikki flickered straight up to Leader, and
flicked her wrist with the end of the
heather, just hard enough to sting a bit.

'Ouch!' said Leader, flinging the beetle-
imp away into the meadow. 'It bit me!'

'You said beetles don't bite,' said
Hogmanay, as Leader peered at her wrist.

'That one did,' she said. 'Where'd it go?'

Tikki popped into view and pointed behind Leader. As she hoped, Hogmanay stared at the place she'd pointed at.

'What? What?' Leader spun around.

'It's there!' said Hogmanay, just as the filly-fae whipped Chrissie's knuckles with its tail. Chrissie squealed and flung the beetle she was holding into the air.

Tikki vanished again, and used her heather sprig to flick Jade's hand, while the filly-fae hunted down Gretel.

'There! There!' said Hogmanay, getting the idea. 'There! No, there!' More imps rained down as the Pixiepackers squealed and darted about. 'It's there!' shouted Hogmanay.

Tikki giggled, and flicked Leader again. The dryfoot boy learned fast.

Then all the beetle-imps marched out of the heather and clacked their fangs at the startled Pixiepackers. They were annoyed with the dryfeet for flinging them about.

'Bite 'em! Chase 'em into the marsh!' yelled Tikki. 'Show us how clever you are!'

The beetle-imps waved their feelers, quivered their wings and rose in a cloud of evil green and red.

'They're going to attack!' yelled Hogmanay. 'Ouch!' He jumped as if bitten, and slapped at the air. 'Ow! It got me!' He grabbed his rucksack from the ground and ran, with the beetle-imps buzzing after him. One of them was giggling, because it felt so clever.

'Well?' said Tikki.

'That's more like it,' said the filly-fae.

8. Into the Marsh!

'Quickly, Pixiepackers,' said Leader. 'Into the marsh!'

'But it's muddy in the marsh!' wailed Chrissie.

'Nonsense,' said Leader, bundling up two tents. 'Remember, Pixie C, *Pixiepackers never whine.*'

'I'll soon change that,' said Tikki to the filly-fae. She flickered ahead of the fleeing Pixiepackers and caught up with Hogmanay McKay in Frog Glade. 'Stop!' she commanded, snagging his collar.

Hogmanay stopped. He looked pleased to see her. 'Tikki, you're *awful*,' he said.

'Thanks,' said Tikki. 'How horrible do you want this camp to be?'

'Horrible enough that Leader will never plan another one,' said the boy.

'All right. Set up the tents in the marsh,' Tikki said.

'Um, where?' Hogmanay looked at the sinister pools of water lurking under the scum.

'I know a perfect camp-spot,' said Tikki. She turned Hogmanay so he faced a pixie path. 'When the others catch up, follow that path. Tell Leader it takes you to a pixie village.'

'They won't believe me.'

'So?' said Tikki. 'It *does* lead to the village where Uncle Sedge and I and the other pixies live.'

'So I'll be telling the truth,' said Hogmanay. 'I never knew anyone could be bad by telling the truth.'

'That's because you've never met a bad fairy before,' said Tikki. She pranced off along the path.

'*Now* what?' asked the filly-fae, flying in Tikki's wake.

'I'm going to make this camp go really badly for Leader,' said Tikki. 'Every Pixiepacker rule is going to be broken. The marsh will be a wreck. Uncle Sedge will *beg* me to go to school.' She skipped on to the pixie village to prepare.

The village huts were small and low, thatched with marsh reeds. Around them were bog-oak seats, piles of compost, and fungus that Uncle Sedge and the other pixies grew for food. The village was protected by DNM spells, which Tikki left in place. She flickered to the green, a beautiful stretch of mud in the centre of the village. Then she cast a Glamour.★

★*This is a spell that makes humans see things that aren't really there.*

In a few seconds, the marshy clearing seemed to become a sunlit glade. The mud looked like a velvet carpet of grass, and the sinister trees took on a sweet and leafy appearance. Flowers seemed to bloom, and birdsong filled the air.

Tikki flickered into the look-see tree, and very soon, she and the filly-fae heard voices raised in song.

'*Pixiepackers smile and sing. They see good in everything. Pixiepackers never whine. They always have a lovely time. Pixiepackers are good as*——Oooh!'

The voices broke into cries of delight as the Pixiepackers saw the fake glade.

'I told you I knew a nice place to camp,' said Hogmanay.

'You were right, Pixie H!' said Leader, patting him on the back. 'It's perfect. How did you know it was here?'

Hogmanay smirked. 'A pixie told me.'

'I'm sure a little pixie is watching right now,' said Jade, tossing her ponytail.

Leader looked around happily. 'Yes, and there she is!' She peered into the look-see tree, pretending to see a pixie there. Tikki stuck out her tongue and waggled her ears.

'I see her too,' cooed Jade. 'Isn't she *sweeeet*?'

9. Pixiepackers Never Whine . . .

The Pixiepackers found it difficult to set up camp.

'I'm not surprised,' said Tikki to the filly-fae, as Jade stumbled over an invisible lump on the ground. 'That mossy bank is really Uncle Sedge's compost heap.'

The tents sagged one way, then another, as Bella tripped over Uncle Sedge's favourite chair and landed splat on top of his hut. 'Ow! These old twigs are really hard,' she said.

Finally, Leader trampled all over the pixies' mushroom crop as she tied the tents to some trees.

The Pixiepackers stowed their bags, and then joined Leader to gather firewood. They accidentally mashed some bracket fungus as they left.

Tikki looked at the mess with delight. She sprang out of the look-see tree and flickered off to Pisky Island, a dank, damp patch of land in the middle of the marsh. Uncle Sedge and the other pixies were there, pulling up forget-me-nots.

'There you are,' said Sedge, as Tikki arrived. 'Pull up these forget-me-nots, but don't disturb the rare heathers and frog ferns. This is the only place they grow. They must be preserved from——'

'Listen, Uncle Sedge,' interrupted Tikki. 'A dryfoot child fell into your hut and sat on your best compost heap.'

'Nonsense,' said Sedge. 'Dryfeet can't see our village.'

'They don't need to see things to wreck them,' insisted Tikki. 'And you know what, Uncle Sedge? *I'm* the one who led the dryfeet there!'

'Oh, go away,' snapped Sedge. 'We're too busy minding the marsh to listen to your silly chatter.'

Tikki poked at a fine frog fern. 'Don't say I didn't warn you.'

Tikki flickered back to the camp, and crawled into Leader's tent to explore a pack of stores. Sugar and salt looked the same, so she swapped them over. She improved the peanut butter by adding peat from the swamp. She was about to put grubs in the apples when the filly-fae stopped her with a flick of its tail.

'Don't ruin good apples!' it said.

'Let's eat them,' said Tikki.

The filly-fae landed on Tikki's hand and snatched a bite of the apple. The pixie and the fetch shared it down to the core, then nibbled bits out of the others.

'The Pixiepackers are coming,' said the filly-fae, spitting out a pip.

Tikki poked her head out of Leader's tent, and watched the Pixiepackers march into the fake glade, carrying armloads of branches. Hurriedly, Tikki and the filly-fae left the tent.

'Make a stone circle, Pixiepackers, then lay out kindling for the fire,' said Leader. She sat on a grassy bank to watch. That is, it *looked* like a grassy bank. Really, it was Sedge's favourite toadstools.

A squishy wet patch spread over Leader's skirt, and the toadstools splattered.

The newspaper kindling got wet. So did all the twigs and sticks that the Pixiepackers tried to light.

When they got the fire started, it smouldered and smoked. Three wading herons sneezed and paddled away to find a safer habitat.

'Let's dance around the camp fire,' said Leader, fanning smoke away from her face.

Tikki popped into view, and winked at Hogmanay McKay. 'Stand aside,' she said, and vanished. The boy backed away, as Tikki blew the smoke right back at Leader. Leader moved, but Tikki made sure the smoke followed her and snaked out to find the other Pixiepackers.*

'Can we put the camp fire out?' wheezed Chrissie, peering through her fringe.

'Of course not!' said Leader, mopping her eyes. 'It's fun. Remember the Pixiepacker Code. *Pixiepackers never whine.*'

---

*Next time smoke follows you at a barbecue, you'll know there are bad fairies about.

Chrissie snuffled. 'But the smoke is chasing us.'

'The pixie girl is playing tricks,' said Hogmanay.

Leader laughed. 'That naughty pixie girl!'

Chrissie coughed. 'I don't like smoke in my eyes.'

'It's part of the fun of camping, Pixie C,' said Leader. 'Remember, *Pixiepackers smile and sing. They see good in everything.* Can anyone see good in this?'

'We could practise smoke signals,' said Gretel. She tore a bunch of green leaves from a rare marsh shrub and waved it through the smoke.

'Very *good*, Pixie G,' said Leader. 'Someone remembers her Pixiepacker Code. Let's signal to the pixie girl.'

The Pixiepackers giggled and

waved branches through the smoke.

Tikki scowled. Uncle Sedge was ignoring her bad deed, and it didn't seem to be working anyway. She wasn't the only one who was disappointed.

'Pssst! Tikki Flicker!' hissed Hogmanay. 'Where are you now?'

Tikki flickered to stand in front of him, then slipped off her DNM spell. 'Here!' She poked him in the middle.

'Don't *do* that,' said Hogmanay, squinting through the smoke. 'You said you'd make this camp horrible.'

'I'm just getting started,' said Tikki. 'Have an apple.' She tossed a nibbled apple at him. 'Hand the rest of them out to the others.'

Hogmanay did so.

'Oh, *good*! Apples!' said Leader. 'Let's roast them.'

'Something's been nibbling at them,' said Chrissie. 'Hog, was it you?'

'Ugh!' said Jade. 'Boy germs!'

'We'll cut those bits off,' said Leader. 'I'm sure it wasn't Pixie H. It must have been a hungry little animal.'

'It was the pixie girl and her flying pony-imp,' said Hogmanay.

'Oh, that pixie girl!' chuckled Leader.

While the Pixiepackers roasted apples, Leader made coffee and put in some sugar. She sipped the coffee, and spluttered. After another sip, she peered at the jar of sugar, then tasted some on the tip of her finger. She poured the coffee onto the ground.

'Now, Pixiepackers,' she said, 'who put salt in the sugar?'

The girls shook their heads.

'It wasn't us, Leader,' said Jade.

'Hog must have done it when he got the apples,' said Chrissie.

'It wasn't me!' said Hogmanay. 'It was the little pixie girl again.'

'Hmmm,' said Leader. 'Let's forget this little pixie girl, Pixiepackers. It's time for some Pixiegames.'

Tikki enjoyed the Pixiegames. She tossed toadstools at the Pixiepackers as they danced around the camp fire, and hid Leader's wand in the look-see tree. Then she threw some bracket fungus on the fire to make it smell bad.

'Do you expect this will earn you that Badge of Badness?' said the filly-fae.

'Of course,' said Tikki.

The fetch stamped its hoof. 'You're just being a pest. I warned you before. Pestering won't impress the hags *or* your Uncle Sedge. Do a *proper* bad deed.'

10. Pixiepackers are Good as Gold . . .

Tikki was hurt. Hadn't she spoiled the Pixiepacker camp? She was about to point this out when she realised most of the Pixiepackers were enjoying themselves, trying to guess what the *little pixie girl* might do next.

'It's not working,' said Hogmanay, sidling up to Tikki. 'They're still *seeing good in everything*.'

'It's Leader's fault,' said Tikki.
'Hogmanay, what makes her cross?'

'*Nothing* makes Leader cross,' said Hogmanay.

'We'll change that,' said Tikki. She dusted her hands. 'I know *just* what to do,' she said.

After that, Tikki concentrated all her tricks on Leader. During an action song, she undid Leader's belt so her skirt nearly fell off. When Leader tried to sit on a tree stump to drink a proper cup of coffee, Tikki pushed a rotten hard-boiled egg under her bottom.

After a while, Leader stopped laughing. 'Tricks are funny, Pixiepackers,' she said, 'but now we've had enough.'

The girls looked at one another. 'We haven't played any tricks, Leader,' said Gretel.

'Well, *I* didn't put peat in the peanut butter,' said Leader.

The girls stared at Hogmanay.

'It wasn't me,' he protested. 'It was the little pixie girl.'

'Enough about the little pixie girl!' snapped Leader. Then she took a deep breath and jumped up. 'It's time she left. All together, now! *Little pixie girl! It's time for you to go home to your toadstool house!*'

The Pixiepackers looked at one another. They liked playing let's-pretend, but talking to an imaginary pixie was going a bit far.

'Come on, Pixiepackers,' said Leader. 'Remember the Pixiepacker Code. *Pixiepackers do exactly as they're told.* Let's tell this naughty pixie it's time to go.' She signalled for the Pixiepackers to begin talking to the pixie girl.

'Little pixie girl! It's time for you to go home to your toadstool house!' they chanted sheepishly.

'She's going now,' said Leader. 'Let's wave goodbye.'

The Pixiepackers waved at an imaginary pixie, and Jade even blew her a kiss.

Hogmanay McKay waved with the rest, though he knew Tikki was perched in the look-see tree above his head.

'And while we're at it,' said Leader, 'let's remember another part of the code. *Pixiepackers are good as gold*. That means no fibs and no more tricks.' She clapped her hands. 'Well, *haven't* we had a busy afternoon? It's time for a pixie-nap.'

The Pixiepackers exchanged glances. They were too old for an afternoon nap.

Leader said, 'If you all have a little nap now, we'll look for rare bog plants later.'

'*Oooh!*' said Bella. 'It's a good thing I brought my *Florapedia!*'

As Tikki watched the Pixiepackers crawl into their tents, leaving Leader to drink more coffee, she had a brilliant idea. 'Now for my *big* bad deed,' she said.

11. They Do Exactly as They're Told . . .

'It's about time, Tikki Flicker!' said the
filly-fae. 'What are you going to do?'

'You'll see.' Tikki danced along a
branch, fished a golf ball out of her pocket,
then dropped it into Leader's coffee.

Leader looked suspiciously into the
look-see tree, but she didn't see Tikki.
She put the cup down on the tree stump,
and went to stand by each tent in turn.

'Have a lovely pixie-nap, Pixie G and Pixie C,' she said at the first one.

'We will, Leader,' said the two girls.

'Have a lovely pixie-nap, Pixie J and Pixie B,' said Leader.

'We will, Leader.'

'Have a lovely pixie-nap, Pixie H.'

There was a pause, then Hogmanay said, 'Um, OK, Leader.'

Leader shrugged and returned to her stump. By then, Tikki had emptied the coffee and turned the cup upside down.

Leader sighed. 'I must be dreaming.' She went to fetch more hot water.

Tikki nipped over to Frog Glade and picked some sprigs of cat-wort.* She tore up the leaves, dumped them in Leader's

---

Cat-wort is a herb that makes people and animals sleepy. Cats love it. So do bad fairies.

mug and added a spoonful of coffee to cover them.

Leader came back with the water and frowned. 'I could have sworn I hadn't put the coffee in yet!' she said. She poured water on top, stirred the drink, and sipped. '*Mmmmm!*' she said, and yawned.

After a few more sips, she put down the mug. 'I might have a little pixie-nap myself, while the Pixiepackers are resting,' she decided. She yawned again, and stumbled to her own tent.

Tikki flickered to Hogmanay's tent, and removed her DNM. 'Hey, Dryfoot!'

'What?' Hogmanay stuck his head out. 'It's your fault Leader made us take a nap! You're making things *less* fun, not more.'

'Trust me, it's about to get very horrible,' Tikki said. 'We're going on an afternoon hike in the fog.'

'What fog?' said the boy.

Tikki beamed. 'Just follow my lead, and you'll see. And so will Uncle Sedge!'

She conjured a ball of marsh gas, and lit it to make it glow. Then she breathed gently onto the glowing ball. 'This is a fog magic spell,' said Tikki. 'There's always fog in some part of the marsh, and my spell gathers it together.'

Tikki breathed out again, and smiled as

fingers of fog sneaked out of the marsh. The layers built up until the mist hovered around her waist. 'Wake the Pixiepackers. Tell them Leader is taking them on a hike,' she said, and flickered to the edge of the fake clearing.

Hogmanay crawled out of his tent. He waded through the fog to the other tents. 'Chrissie, Gretel!' he called.

'Go away, Hog,' said a sleepy voice.

'It's time for our afternoon hike!' said Hogmanay.

'Uh, it's all misty,' said his sister, peering out of the tent. 'Where's Leader?'

Hogmanay pointed to Tikki. The pixie had cast a Glamour to make herself look like Leader. She held the marsh light high above her big blonde head, using the wand she had stolen earlier. She had also stolen Leader's cap to wear.

'Come along, Pixiepackers,' said Tikki, imitating Leader's hearty voice. 'You've had a lovely pixie-nap. It's time for our hike. Quick sticks!'

The noise woke Jade and Bella. They grumbled a bit, but Tikki reminded them that *Pixiepackers never whine.* 'And don't forget, *Pixiepackers are good as gold. They do exactly as they're told,*' she added.

'Sorry, Leader,' said Jade. 'Of course, a surprise hike is fun.'

'I'll bring my *Florapedia*!' said Bella.

'We'll play follow-the-leader,' said Tikki. She pranced off, and the Pixiepackers pulled on their boots and followed. Hogmanay McKay was first in line. As he bounded after Tikki, boots splashing in the marsh, up to his middle in mist, he realised he was having fun!

12. Pixie-Led . . .

Tikki led the Pixiepackers through the marsh, using narrow pixie paths. She strode along, leading them in circles until they began to stagger, squashing plants and frightening frogs as they went.

'Leader, can we rest?' begged Jade.

'*Pixiepackers never whine,*' reminded Tikki. 'I'm taking you somewhere special.' She danced along a narrow path.

On either side were large pools of bog.
'Careful, Pixiepackers. If you fall in here
you might squash some marsh creatures,'
she warned. 'Remember, *Pixiepackers are
nature lovers, kind to pets and all the others*!'
She stopped, and peered around. Aha!
There was Pisky Island! 'We're going to
test our balance now,' she said. 'Follow
me, Pixiepackers!' She hopped up on a

fallen tree and skipped along the trunk. It was easy for her to balance, as her wings helped keep her upright. The Pixiepackers weren't so lucky. They stumbled and wobbled, and stopped.

'I can't see my feet,' bleated Gretel.

Tikki came back over the log. 'Hold onto my belt, Pixie H. Form a line, Pixiepackers, and I'll lead you safely over the bridge!'

Hogmanay grabbed Tikki's belt. His sister grabbed his shirt, and the others joined on behind.

'Step, one, two, three,' said Tikki, and guided them over the bog. Then she shook herself free of Hogmanay's grasp, and led the way into the centre of the island. 'Here we are,' she announced. She looked about, longing to see what Uncle Sedge made of *this*.

But to Tikki's disappointment, the forget-me-not squad had already left the island.

Meanwhile, the Pixiepackers were also looking around. The mist hovered, and they couldn't see much.

'Um, where are we, Leader?' asked Jade.

'This is Pisky Island,' said Tikki, in her own voice. 'There's only one way to get here, unless you can fly, and that's the way we came. The safest thing to do is stay where you are.'

'Leader?' said Gretel. 'You sound different . . .'

'I *am* different,' said Tikki. She tossed the marsh light off the tip of Leader's wand, and caught it in one hand. She removed the Glamour. Then she turned so the Pixiepackers could see her clearly.

'Who are you?' gasped Chrissie.

'I'm the cute little pixie girl you like so much,' said Tikki. 'If you want to know anything else, just ask Hogmanay McKay.' She tossed the marsh light high into the air. 'Catch!' she said. 'And *do* enjoy your stay on Pisky Island. It might be quite a while before you're rescued.'

She giggled, and flickered away, over the tree-trunk bridge and off along the pixie paths towards the fake glade.

The ball of marsh light tumbled into the marsh, and went out with a hiss.

13. Little Pixie Girl

'Very badly done, Tikki Flicker,' said the filly-fae, as it flitted after Tikki. 'Leaving dryfeet children stranded in the marsh is an elegant bit of badness.'

'I haven't finished yet,' said Tikki. She flickered off along the paths until she found Uncle Sedge and the forget-me-not squad. They were scowling over some frog tracks.

'I can't understand it!' Sedge said. 'The frogs are leaving the marsh. Something must have upset them badly.'

Tikki giggled. 'That was me!' she crowed. '*Now* you see what a bad deed I'm doing, Uncle Sedge! I made the camp horrible and because of that the smoke annoyed the herons and the frogs nearly got stepped on and Leader sat on your toadstools and——'

'Be quiet, Tikki,' said Sedge. 'Can't you see we have a serious problem here?'

'Yes, I keep telling you——'

'Oh, go back to the village, you *pest* of a pixie!' said Sedge.

Tikki bit her lip. 'All right,' she said. 'I will. And I'll be badder and badder until you *listen* to me!'

Her uncle turned his back, so Tikki set off back to the village.

'What now?' asked the filly-fae.

'I'm going to make the camp more horrible for Leader,' said Tikki. 'I need your help, so please take off your DNM spell again.'

When they reached the fake glade, all was silent. The Pixiepackers' tents sagged, and the back of Leader's tent had collapsed. Under the Glamour, the real pixie village was a muddy churned-up mess of broken branches, squished toadstools and crooked huts.

Tikki bundled up the big tent and tossed it aside, revealing Leader in her sleeping bag.

'Hello, Leader,' said Tikki, poking Leader in the tummy.

'Hmmm?' Leader yawned and rolled over. 'What?'

'Hello!' said Tikki again.

Leader sat up and stared at Tikki.
'*You're* not one of my Pixiepackers,'
she said.

'No,' agreed Tikki. 'I'm a pixie.' She
settled cross-legged in front of Leader.
'This is the filly-fae,' she added, pointing
to the fetch.

'But . . .' said Leader. 'Are you from the
village?'

'I'm from *this* village,' agreed Tikki.
She pointed at the ruined pixie huts
and removed their DNM spells. 'I live
here,' she added.

'You can't live *here*,' said Leader. 'Is this
some kind of joke?'

Tikki stared at the dryfoot woman.
'I'm a marsh pixie, and that's no joke,'
she said. 'You're camping in the middle
of a pixie village in the marsh, and that's
no joke either. Look around.'

Leader peered through the mist. 'Right, Pixiepackers,' she said. 'This pixie-girl trick has gone far enough! I'm taking you home!'

Tikki sighed. 'This dryfoot is *so* stupid,' she said to the filly-fae. 'She hasn't even noticed her Pixiepackers are missing.'

Leader squirmed out of her sleeping bag. 'Pixiepackers? Where are you?'

'They're out there,' said Tikki, waving her hand. She flickered into the look-see tree. 'I can't see them,' she called, then sprang down with a laugh. 'I wonder if they're having a lovely time, and smiling and singing?'

Leader drew a deep breath. 'Listen, whoever you are. Tell me *right now* what you've really done to my Pixiepackers.'

The filly-fae flew up to hover in front

of Leader. 'She led your Pixiepackers off
and left them in the middle of the marsh.'

'I have to find them!' gasped Leader.
She scrambled to her feet, looking around
the glade. She couldn't imagine why she'd
thought this was a good place to camp.
Even in the mist, she saw twisted and
sinister trees, and creepy tumbled huts. As
for the creature and that strange child . . .

Suddenly Leader remembered Hogmanay talking about the pixie girl and her flying pony-imp. She went cold. It hadn't been a joke! 'Take me to my Pixiepackers!' she commanded.

'Go and look for them,' said Tikki. 'Now I've made your camp horrible, *and* let you wreck this village, *I* have to go to the Abademy to get my Badge of Badness.' She twirled around, delighted with her success. 'Goodbye!' she said.

But before Tikki had taken a step, Leader suddenly slumped to the ground.

'Hey, what's wrong?' asked Tikki, bending to pat Leader's pale cheek. 'They're all right, you know. You've only got to go and find———'

'Tikki Flicker!'

The angry voice made Tikki jump and spin around. 'Hello, Uncle Sedge!'

'Tikki Flicker, what *is* the meaning of this?' stormed Uncle Sedge. 'I come home after a hard day digging up feral forget-me-nots and looking for frogs, and what do I find?' He pointed a trembling finger at the remains of the Pixiepacker camp. 'And what is *that*?' He jerked his thumb at Leader.

'I did tell you,' said Tikki. 'That's the Pixiepacker camp. And this is Leader. I may have given her too much cat-wort.'

The filly-fae swooped down to inspect Leader. 'That's not cat-wort,' it said. 'It's your uncle's sleep-spell.'

'Oh,' said Tikki. 'But *I'm* the bad pixie here, Uncle Sedge, not you.' Then she cheered up. 'I brought the Pixiepackers here to camp as an act of badness. Then I spoiled their camp to help Hogmanay McKay. Then I let *them* spoil the village.

They scared the frogs and birds and trampled the fungus beds, too. Now you *must* see I'm bad enough to go to Hags' Abademy.'

Tikki beamed at the rest of the pixies as they trooped into the ruined village. The pixies stared at her in horror.

'Did you hear that?' Tikki asked them. 'I've done a really big act of badness and I'm going to the Abademy!'

'You're not going to any Abademy,' said Uncle Sedge. He grabbed Tikki by the elbow. 'I'll have no bad fairies in *my* marsh!' he yelled. 'And no dryfeet either.' He spun around and beckoned to the horrified pixies. 'You! Pick up that dryfoot. Take it out to the meadow, well away from my marsh,' he instructed.

Six strong pixies grabbed Leader's limp body and carried her away.

'The rest of you, take these dryfoot things to the meadow and set them up so they look good and proper.'

Several other pixies scrambled to collect the Pixiepackers' scattered belongings, and carried them off.

Ignoring Tikki, Sedge scooped up a handful of mud from the green. He slapped it into a ball, then spat on it. 'Pixie-Fix!' he snapped, and tossed the ball into the messed-up village. It hit with a soggy thud, raining magic-soaked mud over everything. When the mud storm cleared, the village was restored. Only the fungus beds needed replanting.

'There!' said Sedge with satisfaction. 'When that dryfoot wakes, she'll think this was a dream. So you see, your silly attempt at a bad deed has got you nowhere.' He puffed out his scrawny chest.

'Well? What have you got to say to that, Tikki Flicker?'

A tear ran down Tikki's cheek and dripped off her pointed chin.

For the first time ever, she had nothing to say. Uncle Sedge was *never* going to let her go to the Abademy. She'd be stuck replanting fungus beds in the marsh forever.

14. Badge of Badness

'No need to cry.' Sedge patted Tikki's shoulder awkwardly. 'You're not a bad little thing really. All you need is some proper direction . . .' His voice trailed off, as more tears raced down Tikki's face. 'Stop that, now!' he said. 'Saltwater's bad for the marsh . . . I mean, all you have to do is be a good pixie and . . .' His voice trailed off again.

'Aye, Tikki Flicker's quite a problem for you, isn't she, Marsh Warden?' said a cheerful voice. Auld Anni appeared, riding the Abademy's loch-monster, Vetch. Behind her sat the other two hags, Maggie Nabbie and Kirsty Breeks.

'You say you want your niece to have some proper direction, and we're the hags to give her that,' Auld Anni added.

'Aye,' said Maggie Nabbie. 'And a Badge of Badness, too! After all, has she not frightened a grown-up dryfoot and stranded five dryfoot children on Pisky Island?'

'What's this about Pisky Island?' snapped Sedge.

'I forgot,' said Tikki. 'I left the Pixiepackers there.'

Maggie slid down from the loch-monster's back and winked at Tikki.

'Excellent work! Stranding humans is what bad pixies do best! So here you are, lassie,' she said, holding out a dimpled white badge shaped like a golf ball. 'Take it then, it's your Badge of Badness,' she urged, as Tikki made no move.

Tikki gave a terrific sniffle and wiped her nose on the back of her hand. 'Thank you,' she said sadly, 'but it's no good. Uncle Sedge has undone most of my bad act and he'll never let me go to your Abademy. I'll just have to stay in the marsh and try to learn how to be a good pixie, as he wants.' She turned to her uncle. 'I expect you'll have to spend a lot of time teaching me, Uncle Sedge. I don't think I'm very clever at being good.'

Somehow, Sedge did not seem overjoyed at that idea. 'What about those dryfeet?' he growled.

'We'll take them off your hands,' said
Auld Anni. 'As it's our fault they're here.'

'I'll show you where they are,' said
Tikki meekly. She turned and set off
through the marsh with her uncle. The
filly-fae flew gloomily beside her, and
the hags followed on Vetch.

Without all the twists and turns Tikki
had used to lead the Pixiepackers astray,

it didn't take long for the party to reach Pisky Island.

Everyone took off their DNM spells.

Hogmanay McKay was waiting by the log bridge. He goggled at the hags and the loch-monster. 'Whoa!' he said, then scowled at Tikki. '*There* you are, Tikki Flicker. These girls are trying to make me have *fun*! *Do* something!'

'Fun?' faltered Tikki.

'Listen,' said Hogmanay.

Tikki listened as cheerful voices echoed over the swamp.

'It *is*, oh, it *is* blue Bog Heather, Jade!'

'It can't be, Bella. Bog Heather is purple.'

'Here's a Misty-leafed Bog Rose! Oh, and *frog ferns*! They're really rare.'

'I have a specimen bag. Pass me that sharp stick and I'll dig——'

Uncle Sedge's bellow of rage made the Pixiepackers stop in their tracks. 'This is the *limit*!' he bawled at Tikki. 'First you scatter feral forget-me-nots over my marsh, and then you let dryfeet dig up my frog ferns! You *know* I can't use magic to mend marsh plants!' He spun on his heels and glowered at the hags, ignoring the startled Pixiepackers.

'Take her!' he yelled. 'Take her and teach her the proper way to act.'

'It's for the best,' said Auld Anni. She slid down next to Tikki. 'Say goodbye to your uncle, lassie, while Maggie makes a Glamour.'

'But mind,' said Sedge, 'you've got to look after her properly. She's bright, you know.'

'We'll look after her,' said Anni. 'You made the right decision, Marsh Warden.

She'll be happy with us.' She put out her hand, and after a moment, Uncle Sedge took it. 'And now we'll be away. But first . . .' She held out the Badge of Badness. 'Take this, lassie,' she said. 'You have earned it.'

'Ummm . . .' Tikki hesitated, but the filly-fae flicked her wrist with its tail.

Tikki jumped and took the Badge of Badness, and the fetch kicked its heels in the air with joy.

Maggie Nabbie lifted her hand and cast a Glamour over herself, Anni, Kirsty and Vetch. Suddenly, the hags looked like human school teachers, while Vetch resembled a white minibus. Maggie beckoned to the astonished Pixiepackers. 'Come along, bairns,' she said. 'Leader is waiting for you in the meadow camp. It's time you went home.'

The Pixiepacker girls wavered.

'Um . . .' said Jade.

'Who *are* you?' asked Bella.

'She's a teacher,' said Hogmanay McKay firmly. 'Anyone can see that. We'd better get on the bus.'

The loch-monster knelt, and the girls climbed aboard.

'You too, lassie,' said Maggie, 'and you, boy.'

Tikki and Hogmanay scrambled up behind the others.

'Cool!' said Hogmanay. 'What *is* this thing?'

'A loch-monster, I think,' said Tikki. She patted her Badge of Badness. 'Thanks for your help, Hogmanay.'

'Thank *you*, Tikki,' said Hogmanay. 'Who'd have thought a Pixiepacker camp could be so much fun?' He grabbed at

Tikki's arm as Vetch lumbered to his feet and made his way out of Pisky Marsh.

At the very last minute, Tikki turned back to wave. 'Goodbye, Uncle Sedge!' she called. 'Don't forget me!' And around the Marsh Warden's feet sprang a clump of forget-me-nots.

Sedge stared at them for a moment, then he hurrumphed, and left them to bloom and grow on Pisky Island.

A Note from Tiffany Mandrake

*Psst, this is me, Tiffany Mandrake, again.
What happened to the Pixiepackers? you ask.
Well, Vetch carried them safely to the camp the
other pixies had set up around Leader.*

*Leader thanked the hags for returning her
Pixiepackers on their school bus. Then the
humans went home.*

*None of the girls could remember exactly
what had happened on that camp. Leader took*

a holiday to forget her dreams of pixies, flying pony-imps and fake glades. It didn't work, so she started painting pictures of pixies and turned the Pixiepackers' Clubhouse into the Pixiegift Gallery. It's very popular.

The Pixiepacker girls joined the Scouts, and Hogmanay McKay took up golf.

Tikki and the filly-fae feel at home at the Abademy. Sometimes, Tikki visits her uncle, and stops to steal golf balls on the way. Most of the balls belong to Hogmanay McKay. Oddly enough, he doesn't mind.

*

The Abademy of Badness is quite close to where you live. I live in the grounds. The hags know I'm here, and they trust me completely.

They know I'll never say a word . . . and I haven't . . .

. . . except to you.

About the Author

Bad behaviour is nothing new to Tiffany Mandrake—some of her best friends are Little Horrors! And all sorts of magical visitors come to her cosy, creepy cottage in the grounds of the Hags' Abademy.

Tiffany's favourite creature is the dragon who lives in her cupboard and heats water for her bath. She rather hopes the skunk-fae doesn't come to visit again, for obvious reasons.

About the Artist

Martin Chatterton once had a dog called Sam, who looked exactly like a cocker spaniel . . . except she was much smaller and had wings. According to Martin, she even used to flutter around his head and say annoying things. Hmmm!

Martin has done so many bad deeds he is sure he deserves several Badges of Badness. 'Never trust a good person' is his motto.